# Becoming Beautiful

PRAISE FOR *STORYSHARES*

"One of the brightest innovators and game-changers in the education industry."
– Forbes

"Your success in applying research-validated practices to promote literacy serves as a valuable model for other organizations seeking to create evidence-based literacy programs."

- Library of Congress

"We need powerful social and educational innovation, and Storyshares is breaking new ground. The organization addresses critical problems facing our students and teachers. I am excited about the strategies it brings to the collective work of making sure every student has an equal chance in life."
– Teach For America

"Around the world, this is one of the up-and-coming trailblazers changing the landscape of literacy and education."
- International Literacy Association

"It's the perfect idea. There's really nothing like this. I mean wow, this will be a wonderful experience for young people."    - Andrea Davis Pinkney, Executive Director, Scholastic

"Reading for meaning opens opportunities for a lifetime of learning. Providing emerging readers with engaging texts that are designed to offer both challenges and support for each individual will improve their lives for years to come. Storyshares is a wonderful start."
- David Rose, Co-founder of CAST & UDL

# Becoming Beautiful

Sharon Smalls

STORYSHARES

Story Share, Inc.
New York. Boston. Philadelphia

Storyshares
Story Share, Inc.
24 N. Bryn Mawr Avenue #340
Bryn Mawr, PA 19010-3304
www.storyshares.org


*Inspiring reading with a new kind of book.*

**Interest Level:** High School
**Grade Level Equivalent:** 3.5


9781642615340

Book design by Storyshares

Printed in the United States of America

Storyshares Presents

# 1

"Mom, I didn't mean to say that she was ugly... I mean, I just wanted her to be realistic about her chances. I love her just the way she is. She is beautiful in her own way."

Despite my attempts to explain the situation, the look on my mother's face didn't change one bit: disappointment and hurt mixed with a healthy tinge of anger.

"We raised you better than that, Brittney. You're Beauti's best friend. You're the last person she expected to hear those words from."

"I'm sorry. I can go over there and apologize."

"Oh, you bet you will, young lady. That's the least you can do. And apologize to her mother, too. You should have heard the pain in her voice when she called me."

Once again, I was misunderstood. I thought friends were honest with each other. Beauti didn't act like anything I said had hurt her. She had just shrugged and kept looking at her phone.

Beauti was the type of person who never said anything bad about anyone. She was always willing to help people, and she had a very positive outlook on life. Very smart, she tutored many of the students in our class. Most people really liked her.  Even though she didn't have classic beauty features, she still carried herself in a confident manner. I think that's what attracted people to her.

The Miss Libertyville High Pageant was a big deal at our high school. Mrs. Lofton, the teacher in charge of the program, had worked hard to get the program approved. She was a former local beauty pageant winner and thought the program would be valuable to girls interested in learning poise and grace in public settings.

Since I dreamed of becoming a broadcast journalist, I felt the program would help me with public speaking. I was also excited about the opportunity to showcase my singing talent.  So, when I told Beauti that I was thinking about auditioning, she said she was too.

I had looked at her in disbelief. Even though the physical beauty aspect was being downplayed, everyone knew that would count big time.

I didn't recall using the word ugly, but I just stated the obvious: looks would go a long way. I asked her if she understood that. I explained that she didn't fit the typical mold of beauty — especially in a high school that was 70% white. Beauti was extremely dark skinned and wore her hair in a natural afro. And on top of that she was on the chubby side. I had just wanted to spare her the harshness of rejection.

On the other hand, I knew my fair complexion, long hair, and good looks might get me into one of the top three spots.  Guys of different races seemed to be attracted to me, so I felt I could win. I would not have tried if I didn't think my looks could pass the test.

All I wanted for my friend was to see this pageant for what it was. Even though it was presented as an opportunity for all and that it would not be based on appearance, I knew the real deal. People are biased when it comes to physical beauty. That's just the way it is. Why would our high school pageant be any different?

# 2

"Beauti, open up."

I stood outside her bedroom door, hoping she would speak to me. Before I knew it, the door slowly opened. I saw her return to her bed and plop down. I closed the door behind me and thought about what I should say.

"You still coming to the mall with me tomorrow?" I took the coward's way out at first.

She looked at me with eyes that seemed sad, and then she said something that shocked me. "I'm going to win. You know that, right?"

Say what? I was stunned at the sheer confidence and determination I heard in her voice.

"Beauti, I—"

"You don't have to apologize. I know you were just putting your foot in your mouth, as you sometimes do." She broke into a smile.

"I didn't mean it like I said it."

"Yes, you did. But that's okay. I was hurt at first, but I don't stay down long. My faith keeps me strong. God told me I'm going to win."

"But look at what you're up against. Most of the school is white, and—"

"And since you're almost—"

"Don't go there!"

"Well, you are so light you could almost pass, you know."

"No, I don't know!"

I felt the anger rising. I hated when people teased me about my skin color. I often felt like an outsider, especially when my own people jokingly referred to me as being white. Not that I had anything against whites or anybody else for that matter. I just needed to be viewed and accepted for who I was: a proud American. Now she had ticked me off.

"You're just saying that because you're jealous of me."

Beauti's eyes became as big as saucers. "Say what?"

"You know what I'm talking about. Like when we go to the mall and the guys give me all the attention. I watch how you react."

"I don't know what you're talking about, Britt."

"Yes, you do. I see how sad you look when they're not paying attention to you. Which, by the way, proves my point.  We're all being judged by how we look."

"Sad? You're wrong about that. What you see is my disappointment in how you act when you get all that attention."

"What are you talking about? There's nothing wrong with how I act."

"It's really pitiful. A couple of years ago, when you were overweight, with pimples and crooked teeth, no one would look at you. You were the one who looked sad and miserable. Now that you've changed, you act so foolish, batting your eyelashes and acting like you're God's gift to men."

"I cannot believe you just said that."

There was a long moment of silence. I felt bad about lashing out at my friend, but I didn't like the things she had said to me, either.

Apparently Beauti regretted her words as well.  She spoke first.

"I'm sorry if I hurt your feelings. Listen, none of that matters. Besides, we're getting off the point, which is that you don't like being labeled any more than I do. And yet you have the nerve to try to place limits on me because I don't look like everyone else. It doesn't feel good when it's done to you, does it?"

I remained quiet for a moment. She was right. But win?  She must be living in some fantasy world if she believed that. But it was time to calm the waters.

"You're right. I'm sorry for what I said, too. And, apparently, I misread you. I guess it's good you have so much confidence and self-assurance. I'm sure inner qualities will count just as much as outward appearance."  Although I spoke the words, I couldn't convince myself they were true.

"Yeah, going to the mall tomorrow is cool with me."

I had forgotten I had asked, but I was glad she decided to change the subject.

"But just one thing. I saw Miriam after class. She said you told her we weren't going to the mall. Why did you tell her that?"

"You really want her hanging around with us? You see how she dresses — like something out of the 80's. And she walks slumped over as if apologizing for occupying space on earth.  She depresses me. We're going to the mall to have fun... maybe meet some cute guys."

"Brittney, come on! That's so wrong of you. How would you feel if you were excluded from something based on your looks? And so what if she is on the timid side?"

"What is this? Beat up Brittney Day? All right, if you want her to come, call her and tell her."

"It's too late. I don't have her number."

"Well, next time I'll invite her if it'll make you feel better."

"It's not about making me feel better, it's about treating people the way you want to be treated. Sometimes I don't even know why I hang with you. At times, you can do some of the most caring and generous things and then other times—"

Beauti didn't need to finish the sentence. Her sigh said it all. Not willing to take any more criticism, I decided it was time to go.

"Again, I'm sorry. Still friends?"

"Yes. Still friends," Beauti said.

I started to head out.

"Where are you going?

I turned to look at her and saw a warm smile on her face.

"Look, let's not let our differences come between us.  We're bigger than that. Besides, I need you to stay. I have some things I want to try on you."

Good. After all that serious talk, I was ready for some fun.

Beauti was always knitting or sewing something and would try whatever she made on me. A knit cap, or a crocheted scarf.  Sometimes she made beautiful jewelry–mostly necklaces and earrings made with African beads. She was very talented, and I enjoyed being her "model."

We spent the rest of our time laughing and taking photos as we tried on her newest creations. Our Instagram and Facebook friends were in for a treat.

Becoming Beautiful

# 3

On Saturday, when I returned from the mall, my mother was seated on the sofa in the living room. She seemed troubled.

"What's wrong, Mom?"

"Have a seat, Britt."

I sat next to her, expecting another lecture about my hurtful words to Beauti. Instead I got news I had been waiting to hear for over a year.

"Your dad's coming home."

"What? That's great! I miss him so much. Aren't you excited?" She nodded, but I wasn't convinced. "Why don't you seem happy about it?"

"There's something I need to tell you. You see, a few weeks ago, your dad was injured in an accident."

My dad was serving in the military over in the Middle East. I tried not to worry about him all the time. Our occasional video chats always gave me hope that he was going to be okay and would return home to us for good at some point.

"What kind of accident? He is going to be okay, isn't he?"

"Yes, he should be fine."

"Wait — a few weeks ago? And you're just telling me now?  Does Sonya know?"

"Yes, I told your sister when it happened."

"Why didn't you tell me?"

"I didn't want you to worry."

"Mom, I'm 16. I can handle more than you think."

"To me, you're still my little girl. And you certainly act like a little girl sometimes…"

"Mom—"

"Anyway, your sister is grown and on her own. I felt I could talk to her about what I was going through and about what your Dad was facing. I just wanted you to finish out the school year. Since I knew he wasn't coming home right away, I felt it could wait."

"You still didn't tell me what kind of accident. How was he injured?"

My mom looked at me, as if trying to decide whether I could handle the truth. Apparently, she decided I couldn't.

"Honey, you'll see him next week. He'll explain everything to you then. He's handling it with a very positive attitude. I need you to be positive and strong for him, as well."

"So that's why we haven't video chatted in a while."

"Yes, sweetheart. But we're all going to stick together and help your dad through this."

I nodded, not knowing what the future would hold. My mom was putting on a front for me, but I could sense how worried she really was. I couldn't imagine the extent of his injuries, but I would see for myself soon.

"And one more thing. You know your father isn't too keen about you participating in this beauty pageant."

"Mom, it's more than a beauty pageant."

"Whatever. I'm just warning you that he might try to talk you out of it."

"But I thought you said—"

"Yes, he reluctantly agreed to allow you to enter the pageant. But he's not happy about it. I just wanted you to be aware."

As I headed to my bedroom, I hoped that Dad would forget the pageant. There were so many other things I wanted to talk to him about. Besides, it had been too long since I saw him. Now that he was coming home, he might be able to attend the father-daughter dance at school in a few weeks.

I loved showing him off whenever we were in public. He always looked so handsome and pulled together. When we'd go to get ice cream or something, I would watch women admire him.

I convinced myself that whatever the injury, he would get well one day and be back to his old self. Excitement filled my heart at the thought of seeing him in a few days.

# 4

We sat in the bleachers of the school gym. The room was filled with over 100 anxious girls. Only 15 of us would be selected to participate in the pageant. During the preliminaries, we had all demonstrated how gracefully we could walk, said a little something about our hopes and dreams, and had given a taste of our individual talents.

My palms were sweaty, and I found myself nervously tapping my foot. I looked at Beauti, seated next to me. She seemed so calm and peaceful. What was her secret?

Mrs. Lofton stepped up to the mic. She was about to begin calling the names of the contestants, who were to join her on the floor.

I sized up my competition. There were a few girls who might be tough to beat. But from what I had seen, I had an advantage in the talent portion.

Each name she called put me further on the edge of my seat.  When I realized that 10 names had been called and mine wasn't one of them, I started to panic. Again, I looked at Beauti. She was smiling and humming a hymn we often sang at church called *His Eye is On the Sparrow*.

I silently pleaded with Mrs. Lofton to call my name. Now there were only three spots left.

"Would Beauti Tyson please join me on the floor?"

There was an uproar of applause that shocked me. Did she just call Beauti's name? Seeing Beauti head to the floor let me know I wasn't imagining things. Now there were only two spots.

"Only two more names, ladies. Are you nervous?"

Laughter broke out. For me, nervous wasn't the word.  More like puzzled or annoyed. But as I looked at the 13 ladies standing on the floor with the teacher, I realized I couldn't accuse anyone of being racist.  Six of the girls were white, three were black, two were Asian, one was Puerto Rican, and one was Mexican. This was a diverse group, but I wasn't up there.  I almost felt like crying.

After the 14th name was called, I was ready to get up and walk out. Someone have something against me? Why wasn't I chosen? I knew it couldn't be because of my looks or talent. I was very confident in those areas.

"And our last contestant will be..." The pause seemed to last forever. "Ms. Brittney Williams."

I almost leapt out of my seat. My legs were trembling as I made my way down the bleachers onto the gym floor.

"And there you are, our 15 contestants for the Miss Libertyville High Pageant."

As everyone cheered us on, I couldn't help but notice the sadness and disappointment on the faces of the girls who didn't make it. A couple of them were friends of mine and I felt sorry for them.

After our group photo was taken, Beauti and I locked arms and skipped out of the gym.

"We're in!" I shouted.

"Yes we are! But I'm going to win!"

I looked at her and we both burst out laughing.

# 5

When I arrived home from school on Monday, I saw several cars in our driveway. I knew what that meant. Hardly able to contain my excitement, I burst through the door.

Some of my aunts, uncles, and cousins gathered in our dining room. I could see my dad at the dining room table, his back to me. I rushed towards him as he turned around.

Then I froze in my tracks.

He held outstretched arms, ready to envelop me in one of his big bear hugs. "Well, what are you waiting for? Give your old man a hug."

It was as if everything froze in time. I stared at a face that I did not recognize. This was the face of a stranger. The voice sounded the same. The rest of his body seemed the same. But I wanted to know where the handsome man I had known all my life had gone.

"Well, are you just going to stand there?"

He was still smiling. I walked into his arms and gave him a hug.

"How's my big girl doing? You've grown since I last saw you."

"I'm doing good... but I have... a lot of homework and... I need to rehearse for something." I started backing away. "There's a lot of people here to see you. We can talk later."

He seemed hurt. "Sure, sweetheart. If that's what you want. I'll talk to you later."

I rushed to my bedroom and closed the door behind me. Tears streamed down my face and I slid to the floor.

"No, God, no! What have you done to my father?"

How could he smile and laugh when God had done that to him? If we went out together, people would stare. And people could be so cruel. He didn't deserve that.

I got up and wiped the tears away. But the fear and pain overtook me. I flung myself across my bed and sobbed as silently as I could into my pillow.

* * *

The knock at the door startled me. I glanced at the clock. Apparently I had been asleep for a couple of hours. I knew who was at my door, but I wasn't ready to talk yet.

"Sweetheart, can I come in?"

Before I could say anything, the door opened. I had to face him.

He closed the door gently and before I knew it, he was sitting on my bed.

"How's my Pookie doing?"

"Dad, I'm almost grown. You haven't called me that in ages."

"You still are and will always be my Pookie."

I wiped the sleep from my eyes.

"Tell me what's wrong," he said softly.

"Nothing's wrong. I just got tired after studying. I fell asleep, I guess."

I forced myself to look at his face. I had to hold back the tears that tried to escape.

"Tell me what you're thinking."

I thought for a long minute. I didn't want to hurt his feelings — I had done enough of that lately — but I needed to know how he could look at himself every day and not be angry or depressed. How could he be so positive?

I got up the nerve to ask my first question. "How did it happen?"

We must have talked for an hour. When I had all my questions answered, he paused and looked me in the eye.

"Sweetheart, we will all face some very difficult, challenging situations in our lives. But we can never forget that God loves us and walks with us down every road. This accident that resulted in the scarring from my face being burned... that's just another challenge I must face. As I told you, it wasn't easy to accept. I had to work through some anger, but I've accepted my fate. And I'm going to make the best of it."

"But people are so mean. How will you handle the stares? The gossip?"

"What people do is their problem, not mine. Now, it's getting late and you have school tomorrow."

He kissed me on my forehead and headed toward the door. Then he turned to face me again.

"One more thing. About this beauty pageant..."

"Dad, it's not like you think."

"Oh, really? Tell me what I think."

I remained quiet.

"That's what I thought. There's something I never really discussed with you. And I don't want to hurt your feelings, but I've always been honest with you, haven't I?"

"Yes, Dad."

"I'm concerned that you've become a little conceited.  You have been blessed to grow into a very beautiful young lady.  It's important that you don't let that go to your head."

I was stunned. My own father was calling me conceited?

"Why do you say that?"

"It's in your attitude. I know I haven't been around much the past year and a half. But during the times I was home, I noticed that you seemed to be developing a superior attitude toward others. And I've noticed how your friends all seem to be the more popular ones, the most attractive ones."

"That's not true. I mean, look at Beauti—"

He cut me off. "That's another thing. Your mother told me about the situation with Beauti. About how you tried to talk her out of participating in the pageant."

"I apologized, Dad. We're okay now. She knew what I meant.  Anyway, she thinks she's gonna win. Her ego may have been bruised, but she rebounded quickly."

"How quickly she got over it is not the point. You have to stop judging people based on their appearance. That's why you had such a hard time dealing with me tonight. Outer beauty is not what's really important, Britt. It doesn't matter if society seems to disagree. True beauty lies on the inside. I've known some very beautiful women who were made ugly by what was on the inside. I don't ever want that to happen to you. Do you understand?"

"Yes, Dad."

"Goodnight, sweetheart.  Oh, and one last thing. Your mother told me about the father-daughter dance coming up soon. Aren't you glad I'll be here to attend with you?"

"Well… uh… About that. I wasn't planning on participating," I lied. "With all the time I have to put into rehearsals for the pageant, preparing my talk and all that, I just won't have time to concentrate on the dance."

"Oh, really? When you first found out about it you were so disappointed that I wasn't going to be there."

"Yeah, well, I hadn't gotten involved with the pageant when we had that conversation. So things have changed."

"I see." He stared at me as if he could see through me. "Okay, sweetheart. Whatever you want. Good night."

After he left, the guilt and shame crept in. I knew he could tell I wasn't being honest about the dance. Well, it was half true. I did have a lot to do in the next few weeks for the pageant. But if I really wanted to go to the dance, I could have made time to prepare for it.

Was I really that shallow? Was I now ashamed of my dad, the man who always made me feel loved and special, the one who made me feel beautiful even during times in my life when I felt ugly?

As I lay awake, I tried to digest everything he had just said. To be honest, the words hurt deeply. How much was true? I didn't think I came across as conceited or stuck up. But my Dad had always had the ability to see people and situations for what they were. And he would never lie to me.

I had a lot to think about. I didn't want to let my father down. What I had said to Beauti were words I now regretted.

But more importantly, I needed to examine myself so that I wouldn't hurt anyone else.

Looks had always been important to me. I saw firsthand how attractive people were treated better. How some girls were never asked out on a date because they didn't look or dress a certain way.

Up until I was 10, I was the victim of jokes about my teeth, my skin, and my weight. But something happened around the time I turned 13. With dental work behind me, some skin treatments, and a healthy diet, my appearance began to change. I somehow became beautiful.

Before I knew it, boys were looking at me. I liked the attention. It didn't hurt that my sister, Sonya, was in beauty school at the time and taught me some hair and makeup tricks.

Suddenly, guys wanted to walk me home. They invited me to their birthday parties. I went from being one of the nerds or outcasts to being one of the most popular girls in school.

Had I let everything go to my head? Had I become that stuck-up girl who thought she was better than everyone else?

I closed my eyes. My head was beginning to throb. It was time for some much needed rest.

# 6

I waited for Beauti after school.

The pageant was only a few days away, but I had skipped the last rehearsal. I had thought long and hard about my decision. I felt bad that it had come so late in the game, but I knew in my heart it was the right decision.

I wondered what Beauti would say when I told her. As she approached me, I saw she was smiling, but she seemed a bit troubled.

"Hey, how did it go?"

"It went great. Where were you? I was worried."

"That's what I need to talk to you about. I've decided to drop out of the pageant."

"What? You can't do that, it's too late. There's no one to take your place."

"I know. I already spoke with Mrs. Lofton."

"What made you come to that decision?"

"Let's just say I've been doing a lot of soul searching. I had to examine my motives for even wanting to participate. And I didn't like what I found. Beauti, I'm really sorry for what I said to you about entering the pageant. I had no right to make that judgment, and I was wrong. You are beautiful where it counts the most, and that beauty shines from within. Just because your features are different doesn't mean they're not as beautiful. I was wrong to allow myself to get sucked into society's definition of what physical beauty is."

"Well, good for you! Some people never learn that lesson."

"So... Do you think you'll have a better chance of winning now that I'm out?" I joked.

"No, dear friend. I *know* I will win, regardless of whether or not you participate." She was serious but smiling.

I smiled back. "That's a lot of faith."

"To be honest, I'm on my own personal crusade to educate people about what true beauty is. That's what I plan to talk about during the segment where we get to speak from our hearts. Do you mind telling me what you were planning to speak about?"

"The truth is, I didn't really have a message. I was struggling with that portion of the pageant. I was leaning toward discussing how to talk to people to get what you want, but since my father's been home, all I've been able to think about is who I have become. I had to face the person in the mirror, and I didn't like what I saw. But that's gonna change."

"I'm impressed."

"I'll be rooting for you, but I won't be attending."

"Why not?" Beauti asked me.

"I have a dinner date with my dad that evening."

We walked the rest of the way home in silence. I was caught up in my thoughts, still regretting not having gone to the father-daughter dance with my Dad. If I could turn back the hands of time, I would. He seemed to understand, but I could tell he was a little hurt.  Our upcoming dinner date couldn't undo my terrible mistake, but it would set the tone for a new outlook, a new approach to life.

# 7

I woke up Saturday morning to the smell of bacon in the air. That meant Dad was making one of my favorite treats: pancakes and bacon.

I lay in bed for a minute, reflecting on the wonderful time we had at dinner the night before. Despite his extensive facial scarring, my dad was his usual lighthearted self.

Sure, people stared.  But after a while, I didn't care. And he didn't seem to care either.  Although there were no women swooning over him, I realized how much more I admired him.

I jumped out of bed and ran downstairs. Mom was pouring orange juice.

"I was just about to call you down, sleepyhead."

"You didn't have to. The smell of this good food did the job."

"Did you check to see if Beauti won the pageant?"

"Oh my God — the pageant! Thanks for reminding me, Mom. Can you guys excuse me for a minute?"

"Sure, but don't keep your old man and young mother in suspense." He winked at her as he emphasized the word young.

"Sure, Dad. I'll tell you both just as soon as I find out."

I rushed upstairs to get my cell phone but had forgotten to plug it in so it could charge. It was dead. I threw on some jeans and a sweatshirt and ran downstairs.

"I'll be right back. I'm going to run across the street to Beauti's house. I want to hear this news in person."

When I arrived at Beauti's house, she greeted me at the door in her pajamas. From the expression on her face, I could tell she hadn't won.

"Come on upstairs. I was just getting dressed."

I was afraid to ask the question. I didn't want her to have to say the words. I decided to wait until she brought up the pageant.

As I sat on her bed, I saw some new scarves she had made hanging up by her dresser. They were stunning.

"I love the new scarves you made," I told her.

"Oh, yeah. I just finished those a couple of days ago."

"Do you want to try those on me?"

I was hoping to lift her somber mood.

"Sure, have a seat. Oh, and I have a special something I made just for you. Close your eyes."

As I closed my eyes, I felt her place something on my head.

"Okay, you can open your eyes."

When I opened my eyes, I saw a sparkling silver crown. I spun around to face her, and it almost flew off my head.

"You won!"

She broke out in a smile. "Yes, I told you I was going to win!"

We hugged and jumped up and down like little girls.

I stopped to catch my breath. "Girl, you scared me. I thought by the way you were acting—"

"Fooled you!"

"Oh, you wait until I get you back. I'm going to get you real good for that!"

Beauti was laughing uncontrollably, beaming with joy. In that moment, she was more beautiful than anyone I knew.

Through Beauti and my dad, I learned some valuable lessons: the importance of humility, to love and accept people for who they are, to focus on a person's inner beauty and not their outward appearance, and to be confident in who you are.

You don't have to put other people down to make yourself look or feel better. That summed up my best friend. And that's the person I wanted to become. A person full of beauty — real beauty. I wanted to become... Beauti-ful.

# About The Author

Sharon Smalls is an inspirational writer and has loved to write ever since she can remember. From poetry to articles to plays, she uses writing to inspire, encourage, and uplift others. She has had articles published in women's magazines and has recorded a CD of inspirational poetry set to jazz. She is married to the love of her life — Luther Floyd — and lives in Marietta, GA.

# About The Publisher

Story Shares is a nonprofit focused on supporting the millions of teens and adults who struggle with reading by creating a new shelf in the library specifically for them. The ever-growing collection features content that is compelling and culturally relevant for teens and adults, yet still readable at a range of lower reading levels.

Story Shares generates content by engaging deeply with writers, bringing together a community to create this new kind of book. With more intriguing and approachable stories to choose from, the teens and adults who have fallen behind are improving their skills and beginning to discover the joy of reading. For more information, visit storyshares.org.

Easy to Read. Hard to Put Down.

www.ingramcontent.com/pod-product-compliance
Lightning Source LLC
Chambersburg PA
CBHW071226170626
46809CB00005BA/1953